OWLY

A TIME TO BE BRAVE

ANDY RUNTON

An Imprint of

SCHOLASTIC

Library of Congress Control Number: 2020946503

ISBN 978-1-338-30072-7 (hardcover)
ISBN 978-1-338-30071-0 (paperback)

10 9 8 7 6 5 4 3 2 1 21 22 23 24 25

Printed in China 62
First edition, December 2021
Edited by Megan Peace
Book design by Phil Falco
Publisher: David Saylor

FOR MY MOM

THANK YOU FOR
TEACHING ME
THAT BEING KIND
IS THE BRAVEST
THING YOU CAN BE

Fairy Tales

OWLY

OWLY IS SHARING ONE OF HIS FAVORITE BOOKS WITH HIS FRIENDS.
!
Fairy Tales

THE SCARY, SCARY DRAGON & THE BRAVE, BRAVE KNIGHT

THAT SOUNDS SCARY, OWLY.

Fairy Tales

IT'S JUST A STORY, WORMY!
YEAH!

ONCE UPON A TIME, THE BRAVE, BRAVE KNIGHT WAS STROLLING THROUGH THE FOREST.

LITTLE DID HE KNOW THAT DEEP IN THE SHADOWS LURKED...
THE SCARY...

SCARY...

SO EXCITING!
GULP

DRAGON!
A DRAGON!
NO, NO, NO!
!!!

...

THERE'S NO SUCH THING AS DRAGONS.

IT'S JUST A STORY.

I KNOW. IT'S JUST A STORY...

...THERE'S NO SUCH THING AS DRAGONS.

WORMY THINKS
GOING OUTSIDE
IS A GREAT IDEA!

TOYS
?
!
WE'D LOVE TO PLAY BALL!

!
WORMY WANTS TO PLAY...

...BUT CAN'T STOP THINKING ABOUT THE DRAGON.

OWLY KNOWS A DISTRACTION IS JUST WHAT WORMY NEEDS.

THROW IT TO ME, WORMY!

YAY, SCAMPY!
YOU'RE THE BEST!
GREAT CATCH!

OWLY IS HAPPY WORMY IS FEELING BETTER.
HE NEEDS TO FEED THE BIRDIES, BUT HE'LL BE RIGHT BACK.

THROW IT TO ME, SNAILY!

THAT LOOKS LIKE SO MUCH FUN!!!

HELLO?

DO YOU WANT TO BE FRIENDS?

WANT TO PLAY BALL?

I WISH I KNEW HOW.

CAN YOU TEACH ME?

SURE!

THANK YOU!
!

A DRAGON!!!!

HEADS UP, WORMY!
!

WORMY?
WORMY!
WORMY!
LOOK OUT FOR THE BALL!
THE BALL?

BONK!

BOUNCE!

ZIP!

CRUSH!

OH NO!
!

THE BALL WON'T STOP!
CRASH!

NOT WORMY'S TREE!
SNAP!

WHA...?
?

WHAT HAPPENED?
?

YOUR MAPLE TREE...

WHAT ABOUT MY MAPLE TREE?

...THE BALL BROKE IT.

WORMY REMEMBERS WHEN HE FIRST FOUND HIS LITTLE TREE.
A BABY TREE!
WE CAN TAKE IT HOME AND MAKE SURE IT GETS LOTS OF LOVE AND SUN!

OWLY!

SEED

?!

SEED

?

I SAW A DRAGON!

?

I GOT SCARED, THE BALL HIT ME, AND THEN IT HIT MY LITTLE MAPLE TREE!

!

OWLY KNOWS JUST WHAT WORMY NEEDS!
?

?
BUT WHAT ABOUT MY LITTLE TREE...

OWLY WILL BANDAGE UP WORMY'S TREE, TOO.

THERE ARE SO MANY BROKEN BRANCHES...

...BUT OWLY KNOWS JUST WHAT TO DO.

PAT
PAT

!
GREAT JOB, OWLY!

CAN WE KEEP PLAYING BALL?
?

SO, WE CAN'T PLAY?

THAT'S A GREAT IDEA!

OWLY LOOKS AROUND...

...AND FINDS EXACTLY WHAT THEY NEED!

WHAT'S THAT?

THAT'LL WORK GREAT!

I'LL PASS IT TO YOU, SNAILY!

KICK!

ZIP!
OH NO!
BOUNCE!
GREAT JOB, OWLY!
IT WORKED!
WORMY'S ON MY TEAM!

IT'S TIME FOR BED.
NIGHT NIGHT!

OWLY AND WORMY'S
FRIENDS SAY GOOD NIGHT...

...AND HEAD HOME.

LEAVING THE BALL BEHIND...

...FOR SOMEONE ELSE TO FIND.

CATCH!

CA-CATCH!!

OWLY
& Wormy

BRUSH
BRUSH

SHING

SHING SHING
SHING SHING

SHI-SHI
?
SHINGA
?

SHINGA!

GA-GA-SHIN
GA-SHIN
?!
WHAT'S THAT SCARY SOUND?!

SHiNGA SHi...
?

ZZZ
?

OWLY, WAIT!
!

!
I'M COMING WITH YOU!

SHINGA SHING...

OWLY AND WORMY FOLLOW THE SCARY NOISE OUTSIDE.

IT'S COMING FROM DOWN THERE!

SHING!

?!

!
IT'S THE DRAGON! HE'S EATING MY TREE!

OWLY AND WORMY NEED TO TAKE A CLOSER LOOK.

SHING
SHING!

SHING...

SHING SHING!

NO, NO, NO!
!!!

I TOLD YOU! IT'S A DRAGON!

OWLY MOVES CLOSER TO THE SOUND AND FINDS...

!

THE DRAGON!
!

?

?

?

AN OWL!
!

AHHH!
!

SHING
SHING
OWW!
!!!

!

HISSSS!
IT IS A DRAGON!

LEAVE ME ALONE!

YOU WANT ME TO HELP THE DRAGON?

IT IS A DRAGON!
I JUST WANT TO GO HOME!

WORMY SEES HOW SCARED AND HURT THE DRAGON IS...

...AND HOW SAD OWLY IS.

WORMY REMEMBERS WHEN HE FIRST MET OWLY.

?

HE WAS SCARED, TOO.

BUT OWLY TOOK CARE OF HIM.
AND HELPED HIM FIND HIS FAMILY.

THAT'S HOW OWLY AND WORMY BECAME BEST FRIENDS.
WORMY WOULD DO ANYTHING TO HELP HIM.
OWLY...
...I'LL BE BRAVE.
I'LL HELP THE DRAGON.

OWLY IS GRATEFUL TO HAVE A GOOD FRIEND LIKE WORMY.

WORMY WANTS TO HELP, BUT HE'S STILL AFRAID.

GULP

I CAN'T DO IT... THE DRAGON IS TOO SCARY!

BUT HE'S HURT, AND OWLY CAN'T HELP.

WORMY KNOWS HE HAS TO BE BRAVE!

SCRUNCH!

SPRING!

?

TUG TUG!

SHING

YOU'RE FREE!
!

?
I'M FREE?
!
OWLY, COME SEE!
WORMY THE BRAVE!
HE'LL BE SO PROUD OF ME!
?!
OWLY?!
!
IT'S THE OWL!
!

NOOO! STAY AWAY!
!

!
OUCH! MY ARM!

!
WAIT! DON'T GO!
!

STAY AWAY FROM ME!
YOUR TRAP HURT MY ARM!

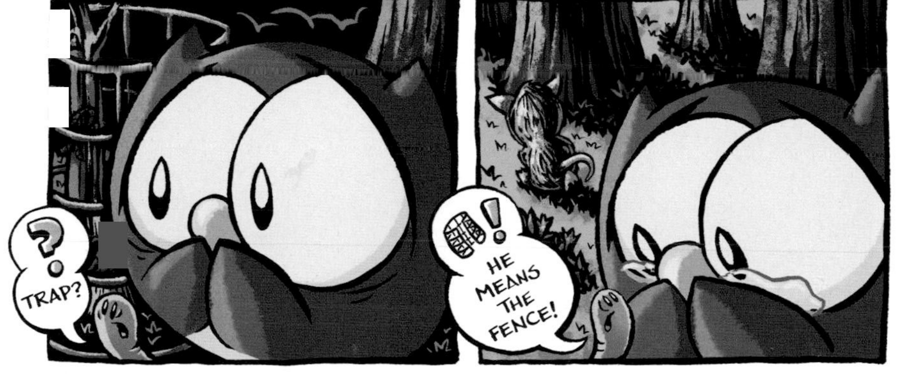

TRAP?
HE MEANS THE FENCE!

!

!

?!
?!
WHERE ARE YOU? COME BACK!

?
WHERE ARE YOU?
?

THUMP!

?
!
COME BACK!

WE JUST WANT TO HELP YOU!

NURSERY
!

CAN YOU HELP US, MRS. RACCOON?

THE DRAGON IS HURT, AND WE CAN'T FIND HIM!
THE DRAGON?

OWLY...

...I DON'T THINK WE'RE GOING TO FIND HIM.

!
OWLY, WORMY, OVER HERE!

?
WHAT HAPPENED TO HIM?
THE BALL HURT MY TREE, SO OWLY PUT UP A FENCE.
!

OH, OWLY...
...YOU DIDN'T MEAN TO HURT HIM. IT WAS AN ACCIDENT.

WE'LL HELP HIM, AND HE'LL SEE YOU'RE NICE!

LET'S GET HIM TO YOUR HOUSE.

HE'LL FEEL SO MUCH BETTER IN THE MORNING.
WILL THE DRAGON BE MEAN WHEN HE WAKES UP?
HE'S NOT A DRAGON, WORMY!
WHAT IS HE, THEN?

!
YOUR BOOKSHELF! PERFECT!

ENCYCL
I-P

!
FOUND HIM!

ENCYCL
I-P

OPOSSUM
(UH-POS-UHM)
HE'S NOT A DRAGON!

THE OPOSSUM IS NORTH AMERICA'S ONLY MARSUPIAL. MEDIUM-SIZED, ITS COLOR RANGES FROM PALE GRAY TO BLACK. BEING NOCTURNAL, IT TRAVELS MOSTLY AT NIGHT TO SEARCH FOR FOOD. IT SLEEPS DURING THE DAY IN HOLLOW TREES, UNDER STUMPS, OR IN DENS BUT DOESN'T HAVE A PERMANENT HOME.

ENCY
ENCYCLOPEDIA

BECAUSE OF ITS LONG, SCALY TAIL, IT IS OFTEN MISTAKEN FOR A LARGE RAT, BUT THE OPOSSUM PLAYS A VITAL ROLE IN A HEALTHY ENVIRONMENT. SOMETIMES CALLED NATURE'S GARBAGE COLLECTOR, IT EATS UP FALLEN OR ROTTING FRUIT AND VEGETABLES, CLEANING UP THE FOREST AND MAKING IT SAFER FOR ALL ANIMALS.

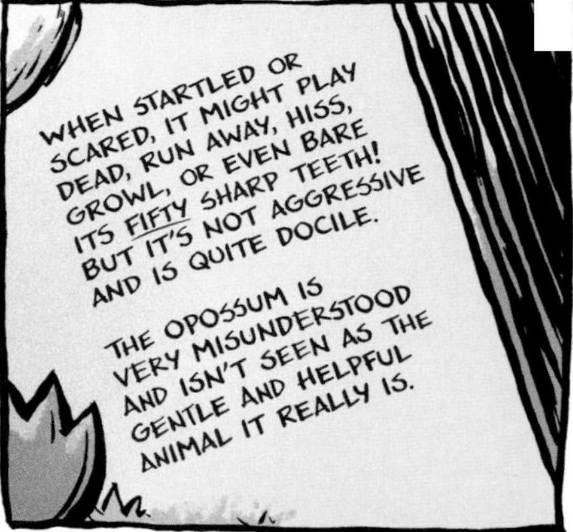
WHEN STARTLED OR SCARED, IT MIGHT PLAY DEAD, RUN AWAY, HISS, GROWL, OR EVEN BARE ITS FIFTY SHARP TEETH! BUT IT'S NOT AGGRESSIVE AND IS QUITE DOCILE.
THE OPOSSUM IS VERY MISUNDERSTOOD AND ISN'T SEEN AS THE GENTLE AND HELPFUL ANIMAL IT REALLY IS.

HE SOUNDS A LOT LIKE YOU, OWLY.

ENC
I-

ENCYCLOPEDIA

Z
Z
Z

I BET YOU'LL BE FRIENDS IN THE MORNING.
ENCYCLO
I-P

!
WE'LL HAVE SO MUCH FUN!

YOU ALL HAVE A GOOD NIGHT.

!
THANK YOU SO MUCH!

!
!
A GET-WELL CARD IS A GREAT IDEA!

GLUE

I THINK HE'LL LOVE IT!
GET WELL SOON!
Owly & Wormy
To!

OWLY

I'M GOING TO GO CHECK ON THE OPOSSUM!

HELLO?
OPOSSUM?
OWLY!

HE'S
GONE!
TO:

PANT PANT PANT
BUMP!

PANT PANT
SHING!

?

THAT LITTLE TREE GOT HURT, AND I SAW THE OWL FIX IT.
AND MY ARM DOES FEEL BETTER.
DID HE FIX ME, TOO?
?
THAT MEANS HE—
=

OPOSSUM?

?
?
WHERE ARE YOU?

?

TO:

?
TO:
BOUNCE

!
OWLY, LOOK!

!
HI!

HEY!
IT'S THE
OPOSSUM!

MY
NAME IS
POSSEY!

TO:

?

TO:

OPEN IT!
To:

To:

To:

OWLY, YOU'RE...
To:

...REALLY KIND! THANK YOU!

CAN WE PLAY BALL TOGETHER?

I HAVE A BETTER IDEA!

OWL
& Worm

!
Fairy Tales

Fairy Tales

DON'T BE SCARED, POSSEY.

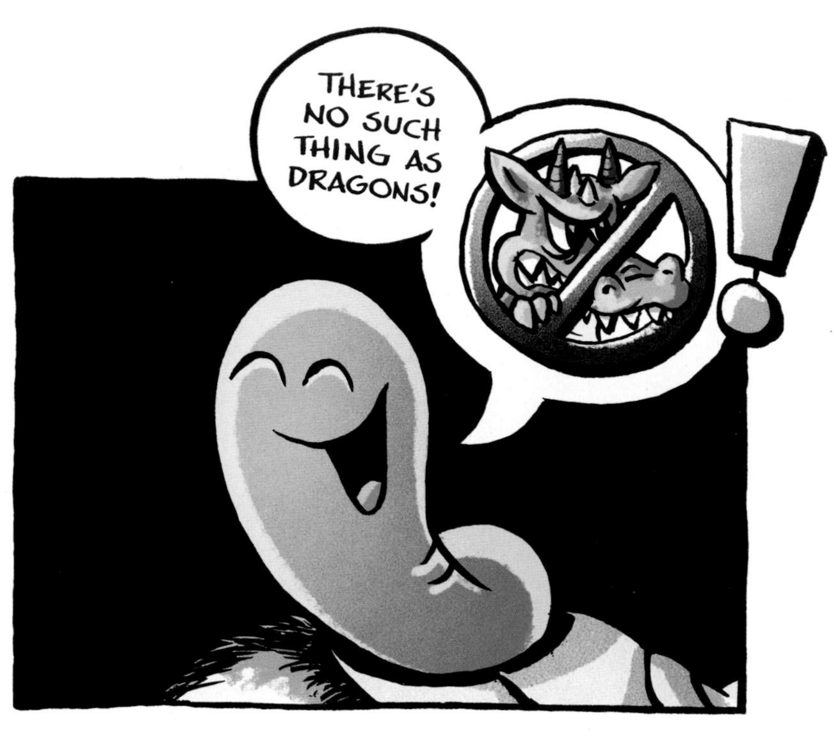
THERE'S NO SUCH THING AS DRAGONS!

Fairy Tales

THE END

The brave Sir Possey defends
Princess Flutter from the scary
Wormy, Scampy, and Snaily dragon!

MORE OWLY ADVENTURES TO COME!

SPECIAL THANKS
TO ALL OF THE OWLY FANS
AND TO MY FAMILY AND FRIENDS
FOR THEIR INCREDIBLE SUPPORT!
IT MEANS THE WORLD TO ME!

THANK YOU TO MY AGENT, BARRY,
FOR CHAMPIONING OWLY, AND TO DAVID,
MEGAN, PHIL, AND EVERYONE ON TEAM OWLY
AT SCHOLASTIC GRAPHIX! YOU'RE ALL AMAZING,
AND I CAN'T THANK YOU ENOUGH FOR YOUR
ENTHUSIASM AND HARD WORK!

AN EXTRA-SPECIAL THANK YOU TO MY MOM,
PATTY RUNTON, FOR ALL OF HER TIRELESS
COLORING ASSISTANCE ON THIS BOOK, FOR
BEING THERE FOR ME, FOR BEING MY BIGGEST
FAN AND CHEERLEADER, AND FOR BELIEVING IN
ME AND OWLY SINCE THE VERY BEGINNING.

AND THANK YOU, DEAR READER,
FOR SHARING OWLY'S ADVENTURES.
HERE'S TO MANY, MANY MORE!
THANK YOU!

ANDY RUNTON

is the award-winning creator of Owly, which has earned him multiple awards, including the Eisner Award for Best Publication for a Younger Audience. The Owly books have been praised for their "charm, wisdom, and warmth" by *Booklist*, and WIRED.com said they are "one of the best comics for kids around. Period." Andy lives in the greater Atlanta area, where he works full time as a writer and illustrator. Visit him online at andyrunton.com.